D1472719

My dog is lost!

My dog

is lost!

EZRA JACK KEATS and PAT CHERR

PUFFIN BOOKS

PUFFIN BOOKS
Published by the Penguin Group
Penguin Putnam Books for Young Readers, 345 Hudson Street, New York, New York 10014, U.S.A.
Penguin Books Ltd, 27 Wrights Lane, London W8 5TZ, England
Penguin Books Australia Ltd, Ringwood, Victoria, Australia
Penguin Books Canada Ltd, 10 Alcorn Avenue, Toronto, Ontario, Canada M4V 3B2
Penguin Books (N.Z.) Ltd, 182-190 Wairau Road, Auckland 10, New Zealand

Penguin Books Ltd, Registered Offices: Harmondsworth, Middlesex, England

First published in the United States of America by Thomas Y. Crowell Company, 1960
Published simultaneously by Viking Children's Books and Puffin Books,
members of Penguin Putnam Books for Young Readers, 1999

1 3 5 7 9 10 8 6 4 2

Copyright © Thomas Y. Crowell Company, 1960
Copyright renewed Martin Pope, Executor of the Estate of Ezra Jack Keats, 1988
Copyright assigned to Ezra Jack Keats Foundation
All rights reserved

THE LIBRARY OF CONGRESS HAS CATALOGUED THE VIKING EDITION AS FOLLOWS:
Keats, Ezra Jack.
My dog is lost! / Ezra Jack Keats and Pat Cherr.
p. cm.
SUMMARY: Two days after arriving in New York from Puerto Rico,
eight-year-old Juanito, who speaks no English, loses his dog and
searches for it all over the city making new friends along the way.
ISBN 0-670-88550-9 (hardcover)
I. Cherr, Pat. II. Title.
PZ7.K2253 My 1999 [E]—dc21 98-37755 CIP AC

Puffin Books ISBN 0-14-056569-8

Printed In Hong Kong

Except in the United States of America, this book is sold subject
to the condition that it shall not, by way of trade or otherwise,
be lent, re-sold, hired out, or otherwise circulated without the
publisher's prior consent in any form of binding or cover other than
that in which it is published and without a similar condition including
this condition being imposed on the subsequent purchaser.

For Sarah and Miguel

My dog is lost!

Juanito was miserable.
Only two days before, on his eighth birthday,
he and his family had arrived in New York,
all the way from Puerto Rico.
Now he was in a new home,
with no friends to talk to.
For Juanito spoke only Spanish.

And, to make him feel even lonelier . . .

. . . his dog was lost.
Juanito's dog had been his best friend
ever since he could remember.
He was a Puerto Rican dog
so he understood only Spanish.
He had been gone since yesterday.
Juanito missed him so much
that he decided to look for his dog
all by himself.

He tried
not to cry
as he looked
in the grocery . . .

. . . the school playground . . .

. . . the movie lobby.

Would he never see his dog again?

He ran to the butcher shop . . .

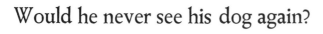

. . . to the laundromat . . .

. . . to the subway entrance.

The busy streets frightened him.
The words the people spoke sounded strange.

Suddenly he saw a big stone building
with wide glass windows.
He read the sign on the window.
There were people inside who spoke his language.
Would they be able to help him?

BANK OF N

AQUÍ SE HABLA ESPAÑOL

"Mi perro se ha perdido," he said.
Mr. Hernández, the bank teller, understood Juanito.
He changed the Spanish words into English
and wrote them on a piece of paper to help Juanito.

Again Juanito went out to the street.
What great, tall buildings!
So many people and so many cars!
They frightened Juanito,
but his love for his dog made him brave.
If he had to,
he would search this strange, new city
from beginning to end.

He held tight to the piece of paper
and started again to look for his dog.

Juanito walked to Chinatown.
He showed the paper to Lily and Kim Lee.
Lily pointed to the crayons
in her little brother's hand
and asked, "What color is your dog?"
Juanito tugged at his brightly colored shirt.

Little Kim asked,
"What kind of hair does your dog have?"
He pulled at his own shiny black hair.
Juanito pointed at a little lady in a big fur coat.

¡peludo!

They shook their heads.
"We haven't seen a red, shaggy dog,"
said Lily and Kim Lee, "but we'll help you look."

They walked to a part of the city
called Little Italy. There they met Angelo.
He made believe he was a dog. He barked and ran.
"Does your dog run like this?"

¡zambo!

Juanito bent his legs to show how his dog ran.

"I want to see a dog that runs like that," said Angelo. "I'll help you look."

Juanito and Lily, Kim and Angelo
walked to Park Avenue.
They met the twins, Sally and Susie,
and told them all about the lost dog.
Sally measured with her hands.
"Is your dog large or small?"

¡grande!

Juanito stretched his arms
as far apart as they could go.

"What kind of eyes does your dog have?"
asked Susie, pointing to her own.

Juanito made his eyes look very tiny.

¡pequeños!

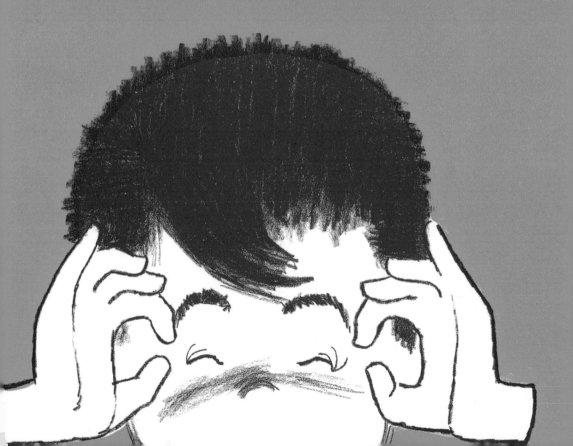

They rode on a bus to Harlem,
where they met Billy and Bud.
"Have you seen a lost dog that's red,
shaggy, bowlegged, and big,
with little eyes?" they asked.
"No," said Billy.
He pointed to the name on his sweater.
Bud did the same, too.
"What is your dog's name?" Billy asked.

¡PEPITO!

As he said the name
Juanito could hold back
his tears no longer.
"Don't give up," said Billy.
"We're all with you.
We'll help you look."

¡PEP

Then they all ran with Juanito

ITO!

WOOF
WOOF

MY DOG
IS LOST

to help him find his dog.

They ran for blocks. They looked everywhere.
They looked and looked and looked.
But there was no sign of a dog named Pepito
that was red, shaggy, bowlegged, and big,
and had little eyes.

"I'm hungry,"
said Sally.

"I'm tired,"
said Lily Lee.

"Me, too,"
said Kim Lee. "It's getting late,"
said Angelo.

"I wish I could speak Spanish," said Billy,
"so I could explain to him."

"We'd better
go home,"
said Susie.

AND

THEN...

. . . they met a policeman.
Juanito showed him the note.
The policeman asked,
"What sort of dog is he?"

"*Of course!*" said the policeman.

"We've been looking for you, too!"

¡jau-jau!

¡perrito mio!

"He's found!" yelled Lily.
"He's found!" yelled Kim.
"He sure is bowlegged," said Angelo.
"He's nice," said Sally.
"I like him," said Susie.
"Hurray!" shouted Billy.
And Pepito said,

¡jau-jau!

Juanito was too happy to say a word.

He and his new friends took Pepito home.

Aquí se habla Español. . . . . Spanish spoken here.

Mi perro se ha perdido. . . . . My dog is lost.

rojo . . . . red

peludo . . . . shaggy

zambo . . . . bowlegged

grande . . . . big

pequeños . . . . little

perrito mío . . . . my puppy

jau-jau . . . . bow-wow

WOOF
WOOF

Also by Ezra Jack Keats